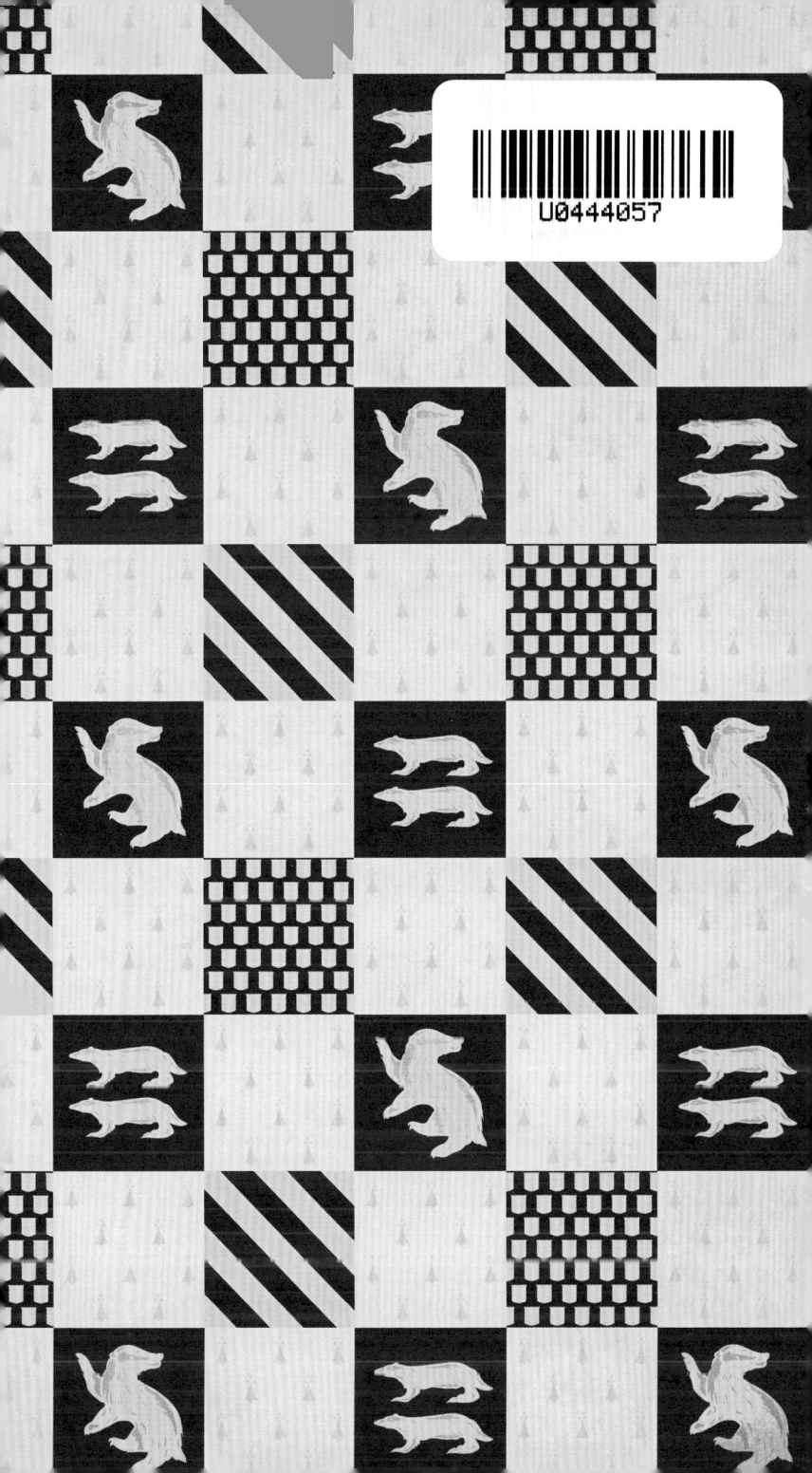

赫奇帕奇

霍格沃茨魔法学校四学院之一，以学校创始人赫尔加·赫奇帕奇的名字命名。这个学院重视忠诚、耐心、勤奋等品质。赫奇帕奇的院徽上有一只獾，学院的幽灵是胖修士。

波莫娜·斯普劳特

斯普劳特教授是赫奇帕奇学院的院长，并且在温室里教授草药学。在《哈利·波特与密室》中，斯普劳特教授向二年级的格兰芬多和斯莱特林学生介绍曼德拉草，并在此后用曼德拉草治疗了被蛇怪攻击的人。

塞德里克·迪戈里

塞德里克·迪戈里是赫奇帕奇的学生，比哈利高两个年级。火焰杯将他选为霍格沃茨的勇士，加入到三强争霸赛中。塞德里克还帮助哈利·波特解开了金蛋的秘密。然而在争霸赛最后，塞德里克被伏地魔无情杀害。

苏珊·博恩斯

在电影《哈利·波特与魔法石》中，苏珊·博恩斯是第三个进行分院的学生。分院帽思考片刻后，将她分入了赫奇帕奇学院。在第二部电影中，吉德罗·洛哈特教授的黑魔法防御课上，苏珊坐在了赫敏旁边。她还加入了洛哈特的决斗俱乐部。

此笔记本属于

哈利·波特

赫奇帕奇学院笔记

美国华纳兄弟公司/编写

人民文学出版社编辑部/译

Dear Mr. Potter: We are pleased to inform you that you have been accepted at Hogwarts School of Witchcraft and Wizardry.

——Letter from Minerva McGonagall, *Harry Potter and the Sorcerer's Stone*

亲爱的波特先生：我们愉快地通知您，您已获准在霍格沃茨魔法学校就读。
——米勒娃·麦格教授的信，《哈利·波特与魔法石》

Platform nine and three quarters? But Hagrid, there must be a mistake. This says platform nine and three quarters. There's no such thing, is there?

——Harry Potter, *Harry Potter and the Sorcerer's Stone*

$9\frac{3}{4}$站台？可是，海格，这一定是弄错了吧。这上面写着$9\frac{3}{4}$站台。没有这种站台，对吗？

——哈利·波特，《哈利·波特与魔法石》

HARRY POTTER

It so happens that the phoenix, whose tail feather resides in your wand, gave another feather—just one other. It is curious that you should be destined for this wand when its brother gave you that scar.

——Ollivander, *Harry Potter and the Sorcerer's Stone.*

是这样,同一只凤凰的两根尾羽,一根做了这根魔杖,另一根做了另外一根魔杖。奇妙的是,你注定要用这根魔杖,而它的兄弟给你落下了那道伤疤。

——奥利凡德,《哈利·波特与魔法石》

HARRY POTTER

I'm Ron, by the way. Ron Weasley.

——*Harry Potter and the Sorcerer's Stone*

对了,我叫罗恩。罗恩·韦斯莱。

——《哈利·波特与魔法石》

HARRY POTTER

Perhaps it would be more useful if I were to transfigure Mr. Potter and yourself into a pocket watch? That way, one of you might be on time.

——Professor McGonagall, *Harry Potter and the Sorcerer's Stone*

也许我把波特先生和你变成怀表更有用些？那你们两个至少有一个人能遵守时间。

——麦格教授、《哈利·波特与魔法石》

Whatever Fluffy's guarding, Snape's trying to steal it.

——Harry Potter, *Harry Potter and the Sorcerer's Stone*

无论路威看守的是什么,斯内普肯定想偷走它。

——哈利·波特,《哈利·波特与魔法石》

HARRY POTTER

This way to the boats! Come on now, follow me!

——Rubeus Hagrid, *Harry Potter and the Sorcerer's Stone*

来这边坐船！快过来，跟我走！

——鲁伯·海格，《哈利·波特与魔法石》

HARRY POTTER

Now what would three young Gryffindors such as yourselves be doing inside on a day like this?

——Professor Snape, *Harry Potter and the Sorcerer's Stone*

天气这么好,你们三个格兰芬多的小孩在楼里待着干什么呢?

——斯内普教授,《哈利·波特与魔法石》

HARRY POTTER

Now, if you two don't mind, I'm going to bed before either of you come up with another clever idea to get us killed—or worse, expelled.

——Hermione Granger, *Harry Potter and the Sorcerer's Stone*

现在,你俩要是不介意的话,我可要去睡觉了,免得你们又有谁想出个好主意害我们被杀死——或者更糟,被学校开除。

——赫敏·格兰杰,《哈利·波特与魔法石》

Tell me what would I get if I added powdered root of asphodel to an infusion of wormwood?

——Professor Snape, *Harry Potter and the Sorcerer's Stone*

回答我,如果我把水仙根粉末加入艾草浸液会得到什么?
——斯内普教授,《哈利·波特与魔法石》

Wicked!

>Ron Weasley, *Harry Potter and the Sorcerer's Stone*

太绝了!

——罗恩·韦斯莱,《哈利·波特与魔法石》

Remember, the Snitch is worth a hundred and fifty points. The Seeker who catches the Snitch ends the game.

——Lee Jordan, *Harry Potter and the Sorcerer's Stone*

记住,金色飞贼是一百五十分。找球手抓住飞贼比赛便告结束。
——李·乔丹,《哈利·波特与魔法石》

HARRY POTTER

Harry Potter must say he is not going back to school.

——Dobby, *Harry Potter and the Chamber of Secrets*

哈利·波特必须保证不回学校。

——多比,《哈利·波特与密室》

HARRY POTTER

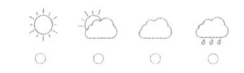

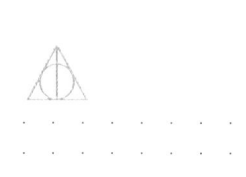

Ronald Weasley! How dare you steal that car? I am absolutely disgusted!

——Molly Weasley, *Harry Potter and the Chamber of Secrets*

罗纳德·韦斯莱！你怎么敢偷车？气死我了！

——莫丽·韦斯莱，《哈利·波特与密室》

HARRY POTTER

I'll ask you three to just nip the rest of them back into their cage.

——Professor Lockhart, *Harry Potter and the Chamber of Secrets*

我请你们三位把剩下的这些小精灵抓回笼子里去。

——*洛哈特教授,《哈利·波特与密室》*

Let's match the power of Lord Voldemort, heir of Salazar Slytherin, against the famous Harry Potter.
——Tom Riddle, *Harry Potter and the Chamber of Secrets*

让我们来比试比试力量吧,一边是伏地魔,萨拉查·斯莱特林的继承人,另一边是著名的哈利·波特。
——*汤姆·里德尔,《哈利·波特与密室》*

Draco Malfoy: "Scared, Potter?"

Harry Potter: "You wish."

——*Harry Potter and the Chamber of Secrets*

德拉科·马尔福:"害怕了,波特?"

哈利·波特:"你做梦吧。"

——《哈利·波特与密室》

Remember what Dumbledore said. If we succeed, more than one innocent life could be spared.

——Hermione Granger, *Harry Potter and the Prisoner of Azkaban*

记住邓布利多说的话。如果我们成功了,就能拯救不止一条无辜的生命。

——赫敏·格兰杰,《哈利·波特与阿兹卡班囚徒》

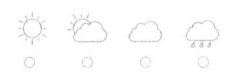

HARRY POTTER

Who is that? Who is... that is Sirius Black, that is. Don't tell me you've never been hearing of Sirius Black?

——Stan Shunpike, *Harry Potter and the Prisoner of Azkaban*

他是谁?他是……小天狼星布莱克,就是他。别告诉我你没听过小天狼星布莱克。

——斯坦·桑帕克,《哈利·波特与阿兹卡班囚徒》

HARRY POTTER

What really finishes a Boggart is laughter. You need to force it to assume a shape you find truly amusing.

——Professor Lupin, *Harry Potter and the Prisoner of Azkaban*

真正让博格特彻底完蛋的是笑声。你们需要强迫它变成一种你们觉得很好笑的形象。

——卢平教授,《哈利·波特与阿兹卡班囚徒》

Turn to page three hundred and ninety-four.

——Professor Snape, *Harry Potter and the Prisoner of Azkaban*

把书翻到第三百九十四页。

——斯内普教授,《哈利·波特与阿兹卡班囚徒》

HARRY POTTER

I solemnly swear that I am up to no good.

——Harry Potter, *Harry Potter and the Prisoner of Azkaban*

我庄严宣誓我不干好事。

——哈利·波特,《哈利·波特与阿兹卡班囚徒》

You know the laws, Miss Granger. You must not be seen, and you would do well, I feel, to return before this last chime. If not, the consequences are too ghastly to discuss.

——Professor Dumbledore, *Harry Potter and the Prisoner of Azkaban*

格兰杰小姐,你知道规则。你们千万不能被人看见,你们会成功的,我觉得,能在午夜钟响之前回来。如果失败,后果将严重得不堪设想。

——邓布利多教授,《哈利·波特与阿兹卡班囚徒》

HARRY POTTER

Expecto Patronum!

——Harry Potter, *Harry Potter and the Prisoner of Azkaban*

呼神护卫!

——哈利·波特,《哈利·波特与阿兹卡班囚徒》

HARRY POTTER

Alastor Moody. Ex-Auror, Ministry malcontent, and your new Defense Against the Dark Arts teacher.

——Professor Moody, *Harry Potter and the Goblet of Fire*

阿拉斯托·穆迪。前任傲罗,魔法部的叛逆者,现在是你们的新任黑魔法防御术老师。

——穆迪教授,《哈利·波特与火焰杯》

HARRY POTTER

Blimey, it's him. Viktor Krum.

——Ron Weasley, *Harry Potter and the Goblet of Fire*

老天爷,是他。威克多尔·克鲁姆。

——罗恩·韦斯莱,《哈利·波特与火焰杯》

HARRY POTTER

The Goblet of Fire—anyone wishing to submit themselves to the tournament need only write their name on a piece of parchment and throw it in the flame before this hour on Thursday night.

——Professor Dumbledore, *Harry Potter and the Goblet of Fire*

这就是火焰杯——每一位想要报名三强争霸赛的同学,都只需将他的姓名写在一片羊皮纸上,在周四晚上这个时间之前扔进这只火焰杯。
——邓布利多教授,《哈利·波特与火焰杯》

HARRY POTTER

Dragons? That's the first task? You're joking.

——Harry Potter, *Harry Potter and the Goblet of Fire*

火龙？这是第一个项目？你开玩笑吧。

——哈利·波特,《哈利·波特与火焰杯》

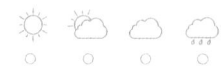

Welcome to the second task! Last night, something was stolen from each of our champions—a treasure of sorts. These four treasures—one for each champion—now lie on the bottom of the Black Lake.

——Professor Dumbledore, *Harry Potter and the Goblet of Fire*

欢迎来到第二个项目！昨晚，每个勇士都被偷走了一件他们珍视的东西。这四件珍宝——对应着四个勇士——现在就在黑湖的湖底。

——邓布利多教授，《哈利·波特与火焰杯》

HARRY POTTER

Earlier today, Professor Moody placed the Triwizard Cup deep within the maze. Only he knows its exact position.

——Professor Dumbledore, *Harry Potter and the Goblet of Fire*

今天早些时候,穆迪教授已经将三强杯放入了迷宫。只有他知道它的准确位置。

——邓布利多教授,《哈利·波特与火焰杯》

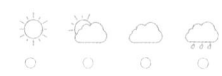

Cho? Um, I was just wondering if maybe you wanted to go to the ball with me?

——Harry Potter, *Harry Potter and the Goblet of Fire*

秋？嗯，我在想你愿不愿意和我一起去参加舞会？

——哈利·波特，《哈利·波特与火焰杯》

HARRY POTTER

You're not going mad. I can see them too. You're just as sane as I am.

——Luna Lovegood, *Harry Potter and the Order of the Phoenix*

你没有疯。我也能看见它们。你的头脑和我的一样清醒。

——卢娜·洛夫古德,《哈利·波特与凤凰社》

Fourteen years ago, a Death Eater named Bellatrix Lestrange used the Cruciatus Curse on my parents. She tortured them for information, but they never gave in. I'm quite proud to be their son.

——Neville Longbottom, *Harry Potter and the Order of the Phoenix*

十四年前,一个叫贝拉特里克斯·莱斯特兰奇的食死徒在我父母身上用了钻心咒。她为了让他们松口不惜折磨他们,但是他们从未屈服。我为我是他们的儿子而感到自豪。

——纳威·隆巴顿,《哈利·波特与凤凰社》

You're a really good teacher, Harry. I've never been able to stun anything before.

——Cho Chang, *Harry Potter and the Order of the Phoenix*

你真是个好老师,哈利。我以前从来没有击昏过什么东西。

——秋·张,《哈利·波特与凤凰社》

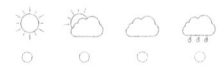

Kreacher lives to serve the noble House of Black.

——Kreacher, *Harry Potter and the Order of the Phoenix*

克利切终生为高贵的布莱克家族效力。

——克利切,《哈利·波特与凤凰社》

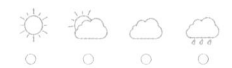

It was foolish of you to come here tonight, Tom. The Aurors are on their way.

——Professor Dumbledore, *Harry Potter and the Order of the Phoenix*

你今晚到这里来是愚蠢的,汤姆。傲罗们就要来了。

——邓布利多教授,《哈利·波特与凤凰社》

HARRY POTTER

But this is Hogwarts we're talking about. It's Dumbledore. What could be safer?

——Harry Potter, *Harry Potter and the Half-Blood Prince*

但我们说的是霍格沃茨。是邓布利多在的地方。还有什么地方比那里更安全呢?

—— 哈利·波特,《哈利·波特与"混血王子"》

HARRY POTTER

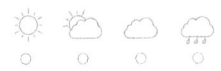

Here we are then, as promised. One vial of Felix Felicis. Congratulations! Use it well.

——Professor Slughorn, *Harry Potter and the Half-Blood Prince*

拿去吧，我说话算数。给你一瓶福灵剂。恭喜你！好好利用。

——斯拉格霍恩教授，《哈利·波特与"混血王子"》

HARRY POTTER

Weasley! Weasley! Weasley!

——Hogwarts students, *Harry Potter and the Half-Blood Prince*

韦斯莱！韦斯莱！韦斯莱！

——霍格沃茨学生,《哈利·波特与"混血王子"》

HARRY POTTER

This vial contains the most particular memory of the day I first met him. I'd like you to see it, if you would.

——Professor Dumbledore, *Harry Potter and the Half-Blood Prince*

这个小瓶里装着一段非常特别的记忆,是我第一次见到他时的情景。如果你愿意,我很乐意和你分享。

——邓布利多教授,《哈利·波特与"混血王子"》

That can stay hidden up here too, if you like.

——Ginny Weasley, *Harry Potter and the Half-Blood Prince*

这个吻也可以变成一直藏在这儿的秘密,如果你愿意。

——金妮·韦斯莱,《哈利·波特与"混血王子"》

HARRY POTTER

He trusts me. I was chosen.

——Draco Malfoy, *Harry Potter and the Half-Blood Prince*

他相信我。他选择了我。

——德拉科·马尔福,《哈利·波特与"混血王子"》

HARRY POTTER

Severus, please.

——Professor Dumbledore, *Harry Potter and the Half-Blood Prince*

西弗勒斯,请求你。

——邓布利多教授,《哈利·波特与"混血王子"》

HARRY POTTER

Dobby has no master. Dobby is a free elf, and Dobby has come to save Harry Potter and his friends!

——Dobby, *Harry Potter and the Deathly Hallows—Part 1*

多比没有主人。多比是一个自由的小精灵,多比是来营救哈利·波特和他的朋友们的!

——多比,《哈利·波特与死亡圣器》(上)

Such a beautiful place to be with friends... Dobby is happy to be with his friend Harry Potter.

——Dobby, *Harry Potter and the Deathly Hallows*—Part 1

真是个美丽的地方,跟朋友们在一起……多比很高兴跟他的朋友哈利·波特在一起。

——多比,《哈利·波特与死亡圣器》(上)

HARRY POTTER

You are a very unusual wizard.

——Griphook, *Harry Potter and the Deathly Hallows*—Part 2

你是个非常与众不同的巫师。

——拉环,《哈利·波特与死亡圣器》(下)

HARRY POTTER

We're in King's Cross, you say? I think, if you so desire, you'll be able to board a train.

——Professor Dumbledore, *Harry Potter and the Deathly Hallows*—Part 2

你说我们在国王十字车站,不是吗?我想,如果你决定不再回去,你可以登上一列火车。

——邓布利多教授,《哈利·波特与死亡圣器》(下)

HARRY POTTER

You have something of mine. I'd like it back.

——Draco Malfoy, *Harry Potter and the Deathly Hallows*—Part 2

你拿了我的魔杖。我想拿回来。

——德拉科·马尔福,《哈利·波特与死亡圣器》(下)

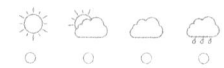

HARRY POTTER

Come on, Tom. Let's finish this the way we started it. Together.

——Harry Potter, *Harry Potter and the Deathly Hallows*—Part 2

行了,汤姆。让我们有始有终。就我们两个。

——哈利·波特,《哈利·波特与死亡圣器》(下)

HARRY POTTER

Professor Dumbledore: "Lily? After all this time?"

Professor Snape: "Always."

——*Harry Potter and the Deathly Hallows*—Part 2

邓布利多教授:"莉莉?这么长时间了还是这样?"

斯内普教授:"一直是这样。"

——《哈利·波特与死亡圣器》(下)

Published by arrangement with Insight Editions, LP, 800 A Street, San Rafael, CA 94901, USA, www.insighteditions.com
No Part of this book may be reproduced in any form without written permission from the publisher.
Copyright © 2020 Warner Bros. Entertainment Inc.
HARRY POTTER characters, names and related indicia are © & ™ Warner Bros. Entertainment Inc. WB SHIELD: © & ™ WBEI.
WIZARDING WORLD trademark and logo © & ™ Warner Bros. Entertainment Inc. Publishing Rights © JKR. (s20)

图书在版编目（CIP）数据

哈利·波特．赫奇帕奇学院笔记 / 美国华纳兄弟公司编写；人民文学出版社编辑部译．—北京：人民文学出版社，2021
ISBN 978-7-02 016640 4

Ⅰ.①哈… Ⅱ.①美…②人… Ⅲ.①散文集—美国—现代 Ⅳ.①I712.65

中国版本图书馆CIP数据核字（2020）第194081号

策划编辑	王瑞琴
责任编辑	马　博
美术编辑	刘　静
责任印制	宋佳月

出版发行	人民文学出版社
社　　址	北京市朝内大街166号
邮政编码	100705
网　　址	http://www.rw-cn.com
印　　刷	上海中华印刷有限公司
经　　销	全国新华书店等
字　　数	10千字
开　　本	640毫米×960毫米　1/32
印　　张	6
印　　数	1—5000
版　　次	2021年4月北京第1版
印　　次	2021年4月第1次印刷
书　　号	978-7-02-016640-4
定　　价	88.00元

如有印装质量问题，请与本社图书销售中心调换。电话：010-65233595

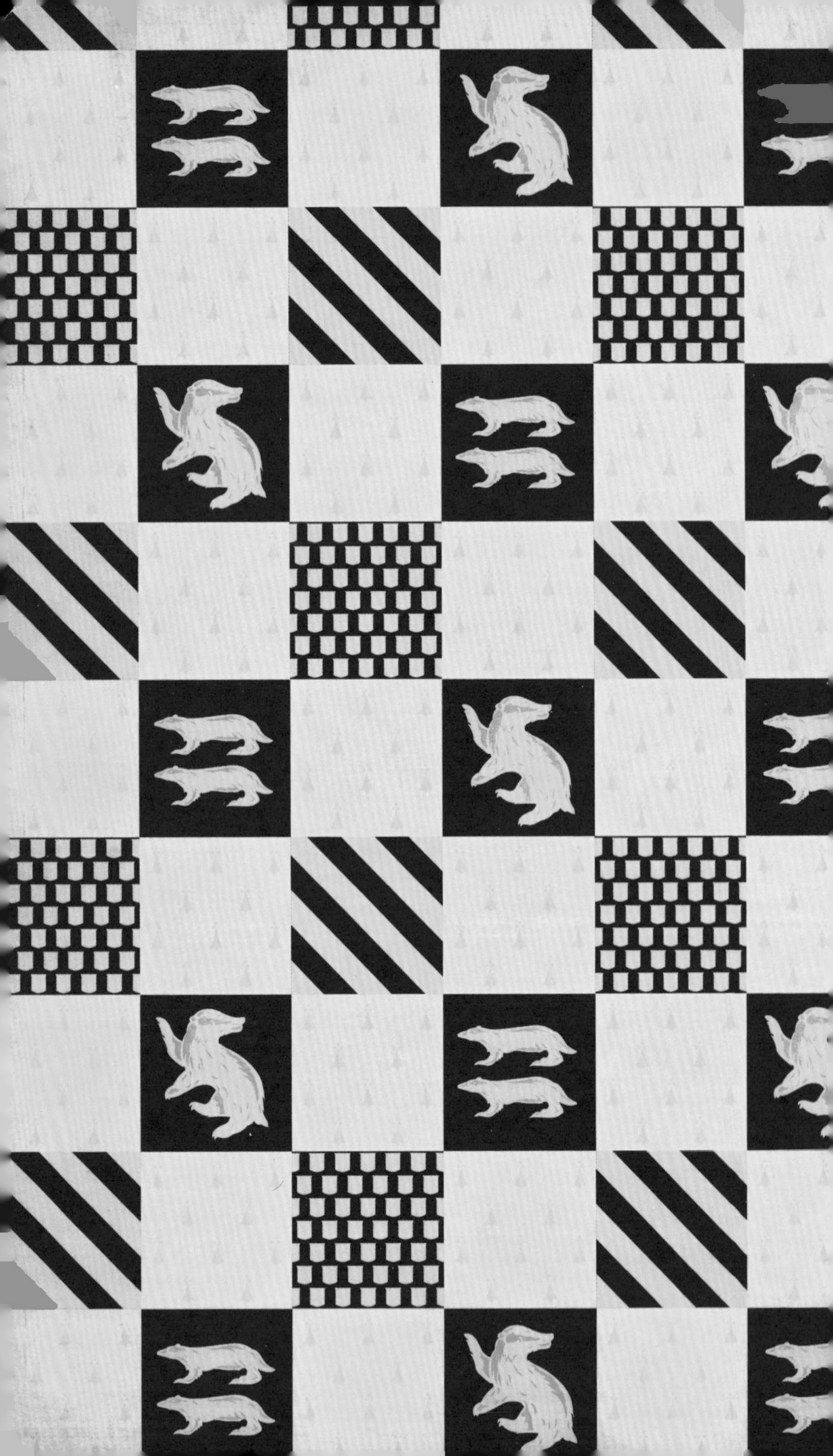